D0916897

THE SERVANT

ROBIN MAUGHAM was born Robert Cecil Romer Maugham in 1916, the son of Frederic Maugham, 1st Viscount Maugham, and Helen Romer, and nephew of the famous author W. Somerset Maugham. Educated at Eton and Cambridge, Maugham trained as a barrister but instead decided to follow in his uncle's footsteps and pursue a career in literature.

Maugham served with distinction in World War II in North Africa, where he reportedly saved the lives of 40 men and sustained a head injury that resulted in blackouts. While convalescing from his wounds, Maugham wrote his first book, *Come to Dust* (1945), which drew on his war experiences. The book was praised by Graham Greene and sold well, convincing Maugham to continue writing full time. Over the next thirty years, Maugham would be one of England's most popular writers, publishing some twenty volumes of fiction and a dozen nonfiction works, including travel writing, biographies of his uncle, and the autobiography *Escape from the Shadows* (1972), which dealt frankly with the three 'shadows' over Maugham's life: his father, his uncle, and his own homosexuality. Maugham was also a prolific playwright, writing scripts for stage, radio, and television.

Among his many works, highlights include the classic novella *The Servant* (1948), memorably filmed by Joseph Losey in 1963; *Line on Ginger* (1949), filmed as *The Intruder* (1953); *The Wrong People* (1967), a controversial novel dealing with pederasty and initially published pseudonymously, and *The Link: A Victorian Mystery* (1969), loosely based on the real-life Tichborne case.

On the death of his father in 1958, Maugham succeeded to the viscountcy, becoming the 2nd Viscount Maugham. His first speech in the House of Lords drew attention to the subject of human trafficking and led to a book on the subject, *The Slaves of Timbuktu* (1961). He travelled widely, living for ten years on the island of Ibiza, but towards the end of his life his health deteriorated due to diabetes and alcoholism. He died in Brighton in 1981.

By Robin Maugham

Fiction
The Servant (1948)*
Line on Ginger (1949)
The Rough and the Smooth (1951)
Behind the Mirror (1955)*
The Man with Two Shadows (1958)
The Slaves of Timbuktu (1961)
November Reef (1962)
The Green Shade (1966)
The Wrong People (1967)*
The Second Window (1968)
The Link: A Victorian Mystery (1969)
The Last Encounter (1972)
The Barrier (1973)
The Black Tent and Other Stories (1973)
The Sign (1974)
Knock on Teak (1976)
Lovers in Exile (1977)
The Dividing Line (1978)
The Corridor (1980)
The Deserters (1981)

Nonfiction, Biography and Travel
Come To Dust (1945)
Nomad (1947)
Approach to Palestine (1947)
North African Notebook (1948)
Journey to Siwa (1950)
The Slaves of Timbuktu (1961)
The Joyita Mystery (1962)
Somerset and All the Maughams (1966)
Escape from the Shadows (1972)
Search for Nirvana (1975)
Conversations with Willie (1978)

* Published by Valancourt Books

THE SERVANT

ROBIN MAUGHAM

with a new introduction by
WILLIAM LAWRENCE

VALANCOURT BOOKS

The Servant by Robin Maugham
Originally published in Great Britain by Falcon Press in 1948
First U.S. edition published by Harcourt Brace in 1949
First Valancourt Books edition 2019

Published by Valancourt Books, Richmond, Virginia
http://www.valancourtbooks.com

ISBN 978-1-948405-44-7 (*trade paperback*)
ISBN 978-1-954321-22-9 (*trade hardcover*)
Also available as an ebook and an audiobook.

Set in Dante MT

INTRODUCTION

I lived and worked with the author and journalist Robin Maugham for the last ten years of his life. He was my friend, mentor and lover.

Not long before he died, he had told me that he needed to check into a nursing home for a routine operation.

One morning in late February, 1981, I'd taken the train to Hove where Robin was holed up in one of the many hospices dedicated to the sick and elderly. I was expecting to see him sitting up in bed, diary in hand, catching up, and planning the months ahead. I was expecting him to point to his ubiquitous bar of alcoholic beverages, carefully concealed in some cupboard, and the first words on his lips to be his usual mantra:

'Do be awfully kind and help yourself to a drink. I do hope you don't mind terribly but I seem to have run out of ice.'

Robin Maugham checked into nursing homes with the same sense of grand optimism as if he were checking himself into the Ritz. There was always a coterie of friends flapping about in the wings, making the usual fuss, carrying books and notes and crates of replenishment. Robin surrounded himself with a whole troop of willing helpers – a leftover of having twelve servants on his old man's estate – in an idyllic house, called Tye, where he'd lived as a kid: secretaries, literary advisors, a cleaning lady, a cook – they were either on hand or at the end of a phone.

Also, during various periods of his life Robin had employed a Barrett, the name of the character from his novel *The Servant*. In certain ways my partner lived out in real time, the life about which he wrote in his most famous book. His Barrett was there to mollify and control him, up to a point. It was a job I could not do and was not expected to do.

The last time I'd seen my partner he was on the doorstep of his house in Brighton with Barrett peering over his shoulder. Suddenly Robin had looked as if he wanted to tell me something vital. He gave a hesitant smile and then blurted out one sentence which I shall never forget:

'You're my only grip on life, William,' he'd said.

I didn't even have the chance to give him a departing embrace because Barrett was in the way. Our last farewell had been cut short – as if the doors had been slammed shut as his train had begun to steam out of the station, he give me a last frantic wave, goodbye.

When I arrived at the nursing home that gloomy afternoon in late February, I was shocked. Instead of the big 'Hurray!' Robin lay unconscious in bed. And soon I realised that he hadn't got long to live.

I found out later that the doctors had warned him that an operation could be risky but he had ignored their advice. For, once again, Robin Maugham was seeking oblivion.

What is little known about the writer is that not only did he suffer from numerous medical ailments, such as diabetes; arrhythmia; shrapnel in the skull from a tank explosion during World War II; he also suffered from a condition that has only recently been better understood, which professional psychologists now call DID or Dissociative Identity Disorder. It is defined as a condition wherein a person's identity is fragmented into two or more distinct personality states. In fact, Robin himself mentions the existence of an alter, who he calls Tommy, thirty-seven times in his autobiography, aptly titled *Escape from the Shadows*. In that book he details several incidences of complete blackout. He describes the experience thus: 'During the periods of my attacks of amnesia, which sometimes last for twenty-four hours, it was the other half of my nature, the half which I called Tommy, who took over. From books on psychology I had discovered that this condition was known as "disassociation of personality". Two different characters now inhabited my body.'

Over the years, Robin had suffered from depression; I was aware of that fact; though I had no idea how deep his psychological trauma went, nor what had caused it.

Originally, Tommy had been the creation of his mama's vivid imagination. He was a ne'er-do-well character, a little rogue she had invented to fill the bedtime stories which she told her little son, Robin, whom she considered to be a rather docile, weak little boy who had appeared rather too late into the Maugham fray for comfort. Tommy was her opportunity to indulge herself with her own longing for freedom and for the unconventional.

Whereas Robin was terrified of his father, the aloof Lord Chancellor, Tommy could cock a snook at the old boy and get away with it without feeling the least bit of guilt.

When Robin first told me about the existence of Tommy, I put it down to too much vino and the pressure of work. I never really took it for real. It was only after I began to seriously investigate his life, and especially when I began my search for his lost notebooks in 1992, that the reality of his condition truly dawned on me.

Children have invisible friends, that's for sure, but when they get older they vanish. Tommy never did. For whatever reason, Robin held on to him. He would appear in his mind during his darkest hours.

As the years passed and his health declined further, Robin's dependency on a servant became an extension of his psychological dependency on Tommy. The relationship reached a kind of symbiosis where one could not do without the other.

He often said that if he hadn't had a mental problem he would probably never have written a word and indeed it was this very pathology which provided much of the source material that drove Robin's creative life. It was as though through his writing he could, at least for a while, dispel the demons that troubled him.

The theme of duality runs through many of his works; particularly so in his novel *The Man with Two Shadows*, where his main character, an intelligence operative, struggles with the fear that he is somehow being taken over by another self and finally believes he is going insane.

However, it is with *The Servant* that Robin Maugham comes into his own, so to speak. It is in this work that he somehow manages to separate the various warring factors of his own personality into a wholly believable world.

Yet, *The Servant* is almost like the draft of a bigger novel. Its economy makes it seem almost rough and unresolved; but it is that very emptiness which begs us to answer its unanswered equations for ourselves; as the author himself could only try to fill the gaps which opened up before him in his own life. In this ironic way *The*

Servant is his most subtle and fulfilled work – it is also his most daunting. *The New York Times* hailed it as 'A masterpiece of writing'.

Robin Maugham sets his story amidst the depression of the '50s. Tony, an upper-class gentleman, has returned to England, shattered from the war – skilfully, we are not informed of its psychological impact on him; except in a brief and telling description, when he is attending an annual regimental dinner, the author suggests that even before Barrett's grip had tightened around him, a complete change in the young man's character had already taken place.

'Against the black of his jacket his face looked white and bloated. The curly fair hair which tumbled about his head seemed to have no connection with the mask it encircled, so that it looked like a golden wig stuck on the pate of an old actor. With a slow pompous gesture he adjusted his tie. His hands were trembling. Then he turned away.'

This is again repeated within various stage directorial notes in the recently discovered original 1958 version of his play, which clearly includes a rape scene when the character of Tony experiences some kind of traumatic shift in personality when he violently pins the young servant girl, Vera, down onto the table.

'A shudder passes over him. Suddenly he takes her fiercely in his arms and kisses her brutally. She gives a little gasp of pain . . . She tries to draw away, but he is holding her tightly. He is breathing heavily. He is no longer watching her. His eyes have a withdrawn look – as if he were thinking of something in the past.'

Unlike Doctor Faustus, Tony does not sell his soul for worldly pleasure; he fumbles into the arms of his nemesis like a man with concussion. This is an echo of what takes place in another piece of the writer's creative output, appropriately titled *Enemy*, where the English and German soldiers do exactly the opposite of what they are supposed to do – they make forbidden, subversive love out there in the wilderness; the two sides become one, each surrendering his power to the other.

Seen through this prism, Tony and Barrett are flip sides of the same coin. Their relationship is symbiotic. Further still, here the tale of 'Gods and Monsters' comes to mind. For Barrett, who is indeed Tommy, is only fulfilling the author's ultimate desire for oblivion – for his weakness and failure.

Finally, like all works of this calibre, *The Servant*, though it is placed within a certain period in history, is in fact a classic parable as relevant then as it is today. For, that which serves us, that which we come to rely on so completely that our lives could not function without its intercession, is destined one day to rule over us, or even destroy us. And, as in the plot in the novella, the catalyst that makes us willingly give ourselves up to that which we may have once rejected, will most often be some tragic event which may affect us personally, or collectively; a plague, a war – which will inexorably make us feel that nothing really matters except our survival and with it our comfort from the storm, for then will we be eager to pay any price.

William Lawrence
January 2019

Note: My investigation into the disappearance of my partner's diaries has resulted in my auto-biographical/biographical work, available on Kindle, titled: *The Night of the Secret Self: My Search for the Lost Notebooks of Robin Maugham, A True Story.*

PREFACE

The Servant is the first work I wrote that was wholly fiction. It has had a strange history. When I wrote it I little knew that, for various reasons, it was to become one of my best-known novels.

The Servant first appeared in 1948 in a small edition with an elegant cover, published by the Falcon Press. Its success was immediate. It has since been published in two English cloth editions and in several paperback editions on both sides of the Atlantic. But if my parents had had their way it would never have been published at all. Alas, they were desperately shocked by it.

The story was a 'natural' for the cinema. But in those days it could never have been filmed. Indeed, I had a letter from the film censor of that period saying that a film of *The Servant* could never be made in our lifetime.

In 1958 I adapted the book into a play. Joseph Losey wanted to direct the play and tried to arrange its production in London. However, at the last moment the enterprise failed. Shortly afterwards an American company made an offer for the film rights. It had taken over ten years for the public's attitude to change.

'Provided I can keep the play rights,' I told the company, 'I accept your offer for the film rights.'

But the film company wanted all or nothing, and so the deal fell through. Yet another company now attempted to buy *The Servant* complete with the play rights. Once again I refused.

My obstinacy in this matter has perhaps been the only wise business move I have ever made. For eventually I sold the film rights without the dramatic rights. Joseph Losey directed a script written by Harold Pinter, and the film was a great success. Meanwhile, I still retained the right to have my play produced.

The first major production took place at the Yvonne Arnaud Theatre, Guildford, on September 27th, 1966. Since then other major productions of the play have been staged all over the world, ranging from Stockholm, Berlin and Paris to Madrid and Buenos Aires. Even at this moment, new productions are being planned.

Many people have asked me about the origins of *The Servant*: what inspired me to write it; if it were based on some true incident. In fact, two disparate events in my life fused together to create the *nouvelle*, as I have explained in my autobiography *Escape from the Shadows*.

The first event took place in Dorset, in the summer after the war. My parents' country house near Hartfield had been requisitioned first by a hospital and then by a tank regiment. It was now being restored, so I had moved to a small cottage to recover from the head injuries I had received in the Western Desert. One afternoon, when I was walking on a near-by common, a girl cantered by on a horse. The girl was very blonde, and the horse very black—perhaps it was this contrast that first attracted my attention. I looked at the girl's face—she was lovely, and about eighteen. I walked on the common each afternoon in the hope of seeing her again, but she never appeared. Then I found myself standing next to her in a queue at a bus-stop. I spoke to her, and we soon made friends. I will call her Vera, which is the name I gave to the character I used in my novel *The Servant*. I discovered that she was, in fact, only sixteen, but had already won several cups for riding. By now I was extremely attracted to her. She was wonderfully slim, and there was a sensual look about the lips of her wide mouth. However, I decided she was far too young for me to have an affair with her.

One evening she came to my cottage for supper. It was a warm night. After we had washed up, we went for a walk. We strolled through the woods until we came to a clearing. We stopped, and she lay down on a bank of grass. She beckoned to me to sit down next to her. I looked at the girl sprawled out beside me, all legs and arms. My desire was fierce, but I made no move. Then

Vera began to speak. She told me that one day, when she was fourteen, her riding-master had taken her to this clearing and stopped because he'd said the horses were sweating.

'He lay down beside me,' Vera said. 'He began playing with me, and he got me so excited that when he did it to me I didn't mind ... We'd stop here every day he'd take me riding after that, and he'd have me. Then I got frightened that I was going to have a baby, so I told my mother. She was livid. But if we reported the riding-master to the police I'd have had to have gone into the witness-box. My mother didn't want that. So she went round to see him and frightened him off. He moved out of the county soon afterwards.'

Vera paused and lay on her back, looking up at me.

'So you see, you needn't worry,' she said.

As I stared down at her she stretched up her arms and drew me down to her.

The second event took place a year later.

When I returned to London from abroad I had rented from a friend a small house in Fulham, and there was a manservant to look after it. Again, I will call him Barrett as I did in the novel. Barrett was an excellent servant. Softly moving and soft-voiced, he would glide silently around the house. But there was something about him which made me shudder each time he'd come into a room. One evening Mary Churchill and I had been to a cinema and gone back to the house for a drink before I drove her home.

'If you've got such a thing,' Mary said, when we reached the living room, 'I'd love a cold lager.'

I remembered that there were two lagers in the fridge in the kitchen.

'I'll go downstairs and get some,' I said.

There was no one in the kitchen, but the door of the servant's room, which led off the kitchen, was open and the lights were on. Lying spread-eagled and naked on the double bed was a boy of about fourteen. His beauty and slenderness reminded me of a boy I had known at school. While I stared at this vision in astonishment, a soft voice spoke from behind me.

'I can see you are admiring my young nephew, sahr,' Barrett said. 'Would you like me to send him up to you to say good night, sahr?'

At that moment I could see myself caught in the mesh of a smooth-voiced blackmailer. By this time I had taken the bottles of lager from the fridge. I pretended I had not heard a word he had said.

'Good night, Barrett,' I said crisply, and walked up the stairs.

When I reached the living room, Mary stared at me. 'You look as if you've seen a ghost,' she said.

I tried to smile. 'I have,' I answered and poured out our two lagers.

At the strange moment when these two events mixed and exploded in my mind, I was in Alexandria, staying in a sea-front penthouse which belonged to a friend of mine called Eric Duke. The book is dedicated to him. He is dead now. But I shall never forget his generosity and his kindness to me.

ROBIN MAUGHAM

TO E.D.

CHAPTER ONE

London was blowsy with heat that summer evening; I decided to travel home from the office by bus. I found a front seat on the upper deck and sat staring down at typists and clerks and shoppers pouring along the warm, dusty streets. 'I am thirty years old,' I thought, 'and I have five pounds in my pocket.' Then I felt the despatch case resting on my knees. I rebuked my fancy. 'You've joined a publishing firm,' I told myself. 'If you don't like having to stay in to make a report on a new book, you should have gone back to being a solicitor when you were demobbed.'

At Sloane Square I clambered down and strolled up the Kings Road towards my little house in Oakley Street.

'After all,' I argued, 'there's no reason to be gloomy. At least I'm in their foreign department and get free trips abroad. I'm in good health. I'm tolerably strong. All my limbs are intact. And there's no war on. Touch wood.'

Perched on the slab in the passage was a note from Mrs Toms, the daily.

'A gentleman rung up,' I read, 'I could not quite catch his name. I think he said he was a

Mr Nonimus. There is TWO ORANGES in the cupboard and the geyser is not right. Mrs Toms.'

I was settling down grimly to my work when the telephone bell rang.

'Hullo,' croaked a man's voice, heavily disguised. 'Is that Captain Merton?'

'Richard Merton speaking.'

'Of the publishing firm of Dimmock and Strachey?'

'Yes,' I said, still trying to guess who it was.

'Well, I have to address a most urgent matter to you. My little daughter Phoebe, aged nine and a half, has just written a masterpiece. Now I wonder what you think she should do with it?'

'I give you three guesses,' I said.

'Are you suggesting that my little daughter. . . .'

But then I recognised the voice.

'Tony, you old devil! How long have you been back?'

'I arrived this morning. What are you doing disguised as a publisher? Come round and have a drink.'

'Where are you?'

'I've got a flat in Ebury Street. Do come.'

I looked guiltily at the manuscript on my desk.

'Please come.'

'All right,' I said. 'What's the number?'

As I walked along the Kings Road, I remembered the last time I had seen Tony. It was five years ago. He was sitting on the top of his tank talking to me with a mug of tea in one hand and his map case in the other when we saw a staff car bumping towards us across the desert. We recognised the Brigade Intelligence Officer.

'Here comes trouble!' Tony said. 'Morning David.'

'Good morning, Tony. I've got something to make you sit up. Read this. You're to leave right away. There's a truck leaving from Brigade in half an hour.'

Tony did not open the envelope. He stared down at David.

'Leave? Where to?'

'For Alex, my boy. You've been posted to the Far East.'

'Ha, ha,' said Tony after a brief pause. 'You quite took me in.'

'Read the order.'

Tony tore open the envelope. Neither of us spoke. I knew from David's face that it was true. Tony read through the order. Then he read it all through again. For one moment I thought he was going to cry. It seemed a long time before he replied.

'What about my troop? I can't leave them while the show's still on.'

'If you were wounded you'd have to.'

'Why did they have to pick on me?'

'You've been on a Commando course. That's

the only reason I can think of. The Brig. told me to tell you he . . .'

David's voice changed as he saw Tony's face.

'He was awfully sorry,' he ended lamely.

Tony was silent. I could guess some of the thoughts passing through his mind. Tony had left Cambridge, where he was reading law, to join our regiment as a trooper in August 1939. Both his parents were dead, and he was unmarried. The regiment had taken the place of a family in his life. At last he spoke.

'Thanks David. Oh, and one thing. You can tell that truck leaving for Alex that I shan't be at Brigade for an hour's time and it can bloody well wait. So long.'

Over the air came the order for our tanks to advance. The last time I had seen Tony, he was standing in the desert with his head tilted defiantly to the sky and his eyes full of tears.

The flat was on the first floor. I rang the bell. Suddenly I felt depressed. I had not seen him for over five years; I was afraid that we would find the ties of our friendship broken, so that although we could feel our way confidently to the past, the present would be awkward and the future would lead us apart. I rang again. There was no answer. Then by the dim light on the shabby landing I read, 'BELL DON'T WORK, KNOCK.' I knocked loudly. He opened the door, and I knew that I was wrong. He had not changed. His hair was untidy, his clothes seemed too small for his limbs, and his homely face was creased by a broad grin. I had forgotten his complexion was so fair. The room he led me into was littered with clothes and suit-cases. He cleared away a pair of riding-boots and a pigskin dressing-case to make room for me on the greasy sofa.

'My dear Richard! What do you publishers do at night? You look at least thirty. What will you drink?'

'Whisky. If you've got some.'

'Masses. That is to say I've got half a bottle. But I think we might finish that before Sally comes, and then go on to drink gin, which is more lady-like, don't you think?'

'Who is Sally?'

'Don't you know Sally Grant? She's the girl we're going out with tonight. You'll fall flat.'

'I'm not going out tonight.'

'Nonsense, my dear man. Sally's only coming because I told her you'd be here. I told her you'd lived for six weeks alone with a camel and would tell her all about it.'

'Come off it.'

'This is my first night in London after five years in the bloody Orient, and you won't come out with me. A fine friend you are!'

'I've got work, and you've got a girl-friend.'

'But she's not that kind of a girl at all. Oh to hell with you! Help yourself to another drink and come and talk to me while I have a bath.'

'You don't need a bath.'

'Is this my first night in London or is it yours?'

There was no chair in the shabby bathroom so I sat uncomfortably on the edge of the bath. The enamel had been worn away in patches at the bottom, which looked scabrously dappled.

'I hope I don't catch the mange from this bath,' Tony said as he lay wallowing in the hot water from the geyser.

I decided I had been wrong to think he was getting fat. His limbs were large and muscular; his broad chest jutted in to a lean waist like a miner's. The impression that he was fat was given by his face, which was fleshy-looking, and by his broad thighs.

'Tell me about Sally,' I said.

'Her parents were great friends of mine. She works in the Foreign Office. She's got brown hair and blue eyes. She's twenty-five years old. What else?'

'Are you in love with her?'

He blushed all over.

'No. At least I don't think so.'

'Are you going back to the Bar?'

'I wasn't even *at* the Bar. Anyhow I've forgotten the little I learned. I suppose I shall have to begin being a student all over again. What a sweat! Richard, where shall I live? I can't live here, can I? It's no good my settling down in Cornwall with my dear Aunt Janie. Do you know of a tiny little house I could buy somewhere not too far from the Law Courts?'

'Bloomsbury?'

'I couldn't live up to it. Chelsea is more my line.'

'It's miles from the Law Courts.'

'There's always the Underground.'

There was a loud knock. Tony sprang up from the bath, splashing me with water.

'That must be Sally. Will you let her in and give her a drink? I won't be long.'

When I opened the front door she was smiling.

'You're Richard Merton. I knew it. Tony's still in the bath? I guessed.'

I mixed two gins and vermouth, and while we talked I looked at her happily. She was lovely. Her oval face and her olive skin seemed all the more pale in contrast to her light blue eyes, which changed quickly from seriousness to mischief. Her body was alive with health. Her movements were natural and quick. She reminded one of a young pony. Although she talked in a careless way about Tony, I realised with a slight pang of envy that she was very much in love with him.

'Where are we dining?' she asked.

'Why don't you go to the Savoy?'

'Aren't you coming too?'

'I wish I could. I've got some work . . .'

'Please listen to me, for Tony's sake, please don't leave us.'

'Why ever not?'

'This is Tony's first night in London after all these years. He'll get tight, won't he?'

'Certainly, but not paralytic.'

'You're wilfully misunderstanding. Oh heavens! How hard it is to say the simplest things! Tony's determined to make a big thing of tonight. It's so wonderful for him, coming back. Everything must seem awfully glamorous. Everything. And everybody. Everybody has got a halo just for tonight. I've got a big halo, you see. I mean we used to be good friends. I don't want him to . . . Oh I know it must sound silly. I don't want him to see me better than I am and then . . .'

'You don't want him to propose to a halo.'

'Yes,' she said, looking up at me. 'You've got it in one. If you're there it'll be all right. We'll all have a good party, and no one will do anything they'll regret afterwards. See?'

'All right,' I said, 'I see.'

The next morning I awoke with a headache. The telephone was ringing with vicious spurts by my bed.

'Richard? Tony. How do you feel?'

'Horrible.'

'So do I. I say, was I very drunk?'

'Yes,' I said, 'very drunk.'

'Did I do anything very awful?' He sounded so penitent that I forgave him.

'Not very awful.'

'Did you see Sally home?'

'Yes.'

'Was she very cross?'

'Not a bit.'

'She's grand, isn't she?'

'She is.'

'When can I see you? Have lunch with me Sunday. I want your advice about finding a house. I'd like a tiny house like yours in Chelsea.'

The next two week-ends we spent searching Chelsea for small houses. We discovered several pubs we had never seen before, several mansions, a farm-house close to Cheyne Row, a derelict barge and a disused factory, but no small house to let. Then Mrs Toms heard from a Mrs Jackson, who was the daily in number seven Benson Street, that the owners intended to let it furnished. I had business in Paris, but Tony went round to see them, and when I returned I heard that he was already installed with Mrs Jackson who came in to work from nine to five week-days and from nine to two Saturdays. I went to call on him.

It was a charming little house, two storeys high and two windows wide, with a basement which opened on to a tiny garden at the back. Inside, the walls were covered with a dark-coloured paper patterned with bunches of grapes and scratches of dirt. It was furnished with fumed oak and square armchairs upholstered in a modern material of brown zig-zags and flashes of red on a blue background.

'The inside couldn't be more hideous, could it?' Tony said. 'But I like the shape of the rooms, and it's quite comfortable except for Mrs Jackson.'

'What's wrong with Mrs Jackson?'

'She can't cook. I wouldn't mind that if she didn't get so cross about it. But every time she burns the pudding, she flies into a rage and breaks things.'

'Why don't you get a manservant?'

'I would if I could afford it. I'll look out for one,' he said.

I often wondered what Tony would have made of his life if he had not adopted my suggestion.

CHAPTER TWO

This story is about Tony. Therefore I only want to introduce people whose actions affected Tony. I must resist the temptation to write of events which were important in my life during this period: how I got a rise in salary and proposed to Mary Saunders and was turned down, how I went to Sweden to get some of our books printed, and how I found consolation there. This suppression of events may possibly appear unlikely and eccentric and it may distort the account of my relationship with Tony, because it will seem as if he was more important in my life than he was in fact. It will seem as if I met and thought about no one else. Whereas during this period, although I was fond of him, our casual meetings were only pleasant interludes in the busy life we both led.

The evening of my return from Sweden I walked round to 7 Benson Street. A manservant opened the door. For a moment I thought I had walked into the wrong house. The narrow hall was painted a smooth white and illuminated by the reflection of the strong light behind a tall vase of flowers so that it seemed as if the flowers themselves shed light. Then a prim voice said:

'Mr Tony is expecting you, sir.'

I walked upstairs. The living room was also transformed. The chairs had been covered with a gay yellow chintz which blended with tawny curtains. Vases of flowers stood on the fumed oak table, which was covered with chequered cloth. With its freshly painted cream walls the room looked light and fresh.

'It's charming.'

'You can thank Barrett.'

'Who is Barrett?'

'Haven't you seen him? He's my servant.'

At that moment Barrett entered as if on cue.

'Mr Richard was just complimenting you on the transformation, Barrett!'

'Just a touch of paint, sir, and a little thought.'

He spoke in a prissy, affected voice, and the word 'sir' sounded like 'sahr.' He walked to a corner cupboard and began to take out decanters and bottles, which he placed carefully on a green tray. I watched him while Tony told me his news. He was over six foot, and I was surprised a tall man could move so delicately. His shoulders were narrow, and his hands were long and bony. One expected his mouth to match his features. But in the middle of his sallow face were stuck a pair of rosebud lips, which gave him the look of a dissolute cherub. His lids were heavy and looked oily, I remember. The contrast between his head and his body was disconcerting, as if a baroque angel were stuck on a gothic spire. His age might have been anything between thirty and fifty. I thought he was repellent. But Tony was obviously delighted with him.

'I've given up trying to control him,' he told me later in the evening. 'He just does everything to the house he wants. Don't you think it's wonderful the difference he's made?'

'Does he find time to do any cooking?'

'But my dear man, he's a splendid cook. You must dine with me one night. He manages to procure the most wonderful food. He knows the black market for miles around. I tell you he's the perfect servant. Barrett's the one factor that makes working for the bloody Bar exams worth while. I've never been so comfortable before in my life. The only thing I draw the line at is breakfast in bed.'

'How is Sally?'

Tony blushed.

'Sally is fine.'

'Why don't you marry her?'

'She wouldn't take me.'

'Have you asked her?'

'Besides I'm not even a barrister yet.'

'You've got a moderate income.'

'Oh to hell with you! Let's go to a cinema.'

CHAPTER THREE

I sometimes wonder whether I could have had any influence over Tony if I had been more often in England during those first two years after the war. But perhaps if I had seen him every month or so I would not have noticed the change in him and therefore could have done nothing to prevent it. Yet I was only six months in the Middle East that winter, and when he came to lunch with me the day after my return I noticed the difference. He had put on weight, and there was a coarse look about him which I had never seen before. Mrs Toms had a maddening habit of bringing in each dish one by one, which interrupts conversation, and I had hoped Tony would stay on for a talk after lunch; but he had to get back to Lincoln's Inn for a lecture. His exam was in a few weeks' time. However he had invited me to dine with him on Saturday night. On Saturday morning I ran into Sally in Harrods.

'I want to speak to you,' she said.

'Well, speak away.'

'Oh don't be funny. This is serious.'

I looked at my watch.

'Let's go and have a drink somewhere.'

We settled down in the corner of the bar of the Hyde Park Hotel. I talked brightly about camels and bazaars until two dry martinis were brought.

'Now what is it?'

'I'm losing Tony.'

'Another woman?'

'No, another man.'

I stared at her. She took a sip of cocktail.

'I'm losing him to Barrett,' she said.

I laughed outright. Suddenly she burst into tears. I never know what to do when a woman cries. Luckily I had a large clean handkerchief. While she controlled herself I went to the bar and collected two more drinks. I made her drink them both. Then we each had another drink, and over lunch she told me the story.

Immediately after his return she and Tony had gone about together.

'We knew the same lot so it wasn't difficult. If there wasn't a dinner-party, we'd find some little restaurant and go to a cinema afterwards. That was before he got Barrett.'

'What difference did that make?'

'None at first. But gradually he seemed less keen on going out. I must say Barrett cooked awfully well, so we'd dine at Benson Street. I can't bear the house. I can't explain why. It's clean and smart, but it's somehow nasty. Perhaps it's because of Barrett.'

Her blue eyes suddenly glowed.

'I detest him,' she whispered. 'I wish he was dead. I know that's wicked. But I do. I wish he was dead.'

'He looks like a fish with painted lips. But apart from that, what's wrong with him?'

'He's ruining Tony.'

'What nonsense!'

'It's true. He's found out Tony's weakness, and he's playing on it.'

'What is his weakness?'

'He's lazy, and he likes to be comfortable.'

'Don't we all?' I said.

'Look. It's going to be hard to explain this. Please try to understand. Barrett is wrapping up Tony in comfort. Wait till you go there. He does everything for Tony. He cooks, he sweeps, he makes the cocktails, he turns on the radio, turns on his bath, takes off his shoes. Yes, I've even seen him take off Tony's shoes and put on his slippers because Tony couldn't be bothered to change them himself.'

I laughed.

'He sounds the perfect servant. If Tony isn't careful he'll grow into a fat, middle-aged bachelor. But I don't see anything to cry about.'

'You've seen Tony. Haven't you noticed how much he's changed?'

'He's put on weight, that's all.'

'He's been ruined. Richard, I've seen it. I've seen Barrett gaining power over him.'

'All right, Sally. How?'

'We used to dine at Benson Street. I don't think Barrett minded me at first. It was cosy in the little room. I could see Tony wasn't keen to go out. So we stopped going to the cinemas. We'd just stay by the fire talking.'

I interrupted. 'We're old friends now,' I said. 'So do you mind if I ask a few plain questions?'

She smiled. 'I don't promise to answer them all,' she replied.

'Did you go to bed with him?'

'No.' She took a sip of wine. 'Things were getting on that way. And I . . . well, I'd have let him. But just then he stopped. I mean he suddenly drew back. I suppose . . .'

'No,' I said, 'he's perfectly normal.'

'We were in the living room, and I thought he'd locked the door. But suddenly Barrett walked in. I felt awful. Barrett just said "I'm sorry, sir, to disturb you" and walked out. From that moment Barrett hated me. I know it. You can't imagine how I loathe telling you all this.'

'I can't help much unless you do.'

'The row blew up over a ridiculously small incident. I'm afraid you'll think I was petty. Tony was in bed with a bad attack of flu. I went to visit him and brought some flowers with me. They were lupins, I remember. Cost quite a lot. He was pathetically grateful. I went again two days later. The poor sweet really was quite ill. On the way up to his room I noticed the lupins I'd brought had been put in a vase on the landing. There were no flowers in his room at all, and I couldn't help asking him about the lupins.'

I could see the three of them in Tony's little room.

'Barrett thinks it's bad for me to have flowers in my room,' Tony said.

'Rot,' Sally replied, and went downstairs and brought back the lupins. Presently Barrett came creeping in.

'Good morning, Miss Grant,' he said. 'How do you think our patient is doing?' Then he saw the flowers on the dressing-table.

'I'm afraid we can't allow flowers in our patient's room, can we, sahr?'

She expected Tony to tell him to go to hell, but he said nothing.

'I don't think flowers do any harm by day,' she said, trying to make her voice sound calm.

'I'm afraid that unless the doctor gives his permission I must remove them,' he replied, and took up the vase from the table.

'Put that vase down,' she said.

Barrett looked at Tony.

'Put it down, Barrett,' Tony said after a pause. Barrett did not answer. He put the vase back on the table and walked slowly out of the room. Sally was furious. But Tony was ill.

With an effort she controlled herself. For a

moment neither of them spoke. Then Tony said, 'Please try not to cross Barrett every time you come here. If he goes it'll be a cracking bore.'

'Then I lost my temper,' Sally told me with flashing eyes. 'I've not seen Tony since.'

She gulped down the coffee and stood up. I was afraid she was going to cry.

'I'm off, Richard. Forgive me for being stupid. But you see, I love him. Let me know, won't you. Thanks for everything. So long.'

That evening at Benson Street, while Barrett was downstairs cooking dinner, I tackled Tony.

I expected him to make excuses, and his attitude surprised me.

'Sally really has behaved ridiculously,' he said. 'I've been patient. But she goes on as if Barrett was a re-incarnation of Svengali. Heaven deliver me from neurotic women!'

'I thought you were in love.'

'I'm awfully fond of her.'

'You know what I mean.'

'All right. I'm not in love with her.'

'Anyone else?'

'Certainly not.'

'Just a happy wolf?'

'Moderately happy. I'm not all that hungry, dear man. I like a full night's sleep. How right the French are to make love in the afternoon. In England our pubs shut too soon and girls go to bed too late.'

'You've changed.'

'Now don't you start. Come on. Let's go out and get a drink.'

We wandered round to the pub in Kings Road. We each drank a pint of bitter, and I was just about to suggest a second when Tony said: 'We ought to be getting back. It fusses Barrett if one's late.'

'Damn Barrett,' I said.

'My dear man, he's a perfect servant, and I'm not going to lose him if I can help it.'

'I believe Sally's right. He's gradually getting a hold on you.'

'Bollocks. I'd get rid of him tomorrow if I wanted to. But I don't. I'll admit he's a prim old bore. But he's a bloody good servant, and I'm keeping him. Even if it means taking in his niece.'

'His niece?'

'He says it's only temporarily while she looks round for a job. I need only pay for her food.'

'You'll be having his whole family next. I don't trust that man a yard. I believe . . .'

'Listen,' Tony said. 'We want to enjoy ourselves this evening, don't we? Then do you mind if we don't talk about Barrett again tonight?'

The dinner was beautifully cooked. We had clear soup, Dover sole, steak and onions, and a delicious chocolate soufflée.

'How do you manage it?' I asked.

'Oh Barrett's the king of the local black market.'

At ten o'clock Barrett meticulously laid out a drink tray in the living room.

'Breakfast in bed at the usual time, sahr?' he said, as he turned to leave the room.

'Yes, thank you Barrett.'

CHAPTER FOUR

Those of us who enjoy private incomes, however small, or the affluence of relations, cannot know the insecurity which haunts those who have no money and no refuge. Servants who are completely dependent on their employers for home and wages, who can be ordered to work at any time, and whose environment can be shattered by a broken teapot or a spurt of temper, develop neuroses of their own. Though a servant may be quite fond of her master, she may unconsciously try to worry or irritate him in order to depress him. Her fads and fancies, her fits of sulks, her huffiness and quickness to take offence are all the result of a hidden urge to compensate for the inequality of status. It is the only way she knows of getting on the same level. Or so I tell myself when Mrs Toms is exceptionally tiresome. About the ice for instance.

I cannot afford a refrigerator. When people are coming in for drinks I have to warn Mrs Toms in advance so that she can get ice from the fishmonger around the corner. Perhaps she considers ice a silly luxury, perhaps she dislikes the fishmonger; I have never been able to discover the reason. However, she does all she can to avoid walking a hundred yards to get a few chunks of ice in a jug.

Some friends were coming in to drinks that evening. At two o'clock when I was leaving for the office, Mrs Toms burst in on me triumphantly. She is a wiry little woman with fierce black hair and beady black eyes. In her bursting moods she reminds me of a cavalry colonel about to order a charge. She has an astonishingly loud voice and bandy legs, and she is highly emotional.

'Would you believe it,' she bellowed. 'It's Wednesday. Early closing. Can't get no ice any-where. All the shops shut. And I know you like a piece of ice when you've got people coming. Whatever shall I do?'

'Why not go round to Mr Tony's house? He's got a refrigerator.'

'It's quite a way.'

'It's only the third turning up the Kings Road.'

'Perhaps there won't be none in.'

'Then we shall have to think of something else.'

'I've got the rooms to tidy yet.'

'There's plenty of time.'

'You know I'd never let you down, don't you, Mr Richard?'

'Yes, Mrs Toms, I do.'

'I'd even go down on my bended knees to the fishmonger.'

We were now reaching the stage close to tears.

'I'm sure you would, Mrs Toms. Why not go round at four o'clock? Then Barrett will give you a cup of tea.'

'I suppose I might do that, I suppose.'

I had avoided a scene. I breathed freely.

'I hope Mr Tony will be coming in later this evening,' I said. I knew she liked Tony.

'I suppose he couldn't bring the ice, could he now?'

'He's coming straight from Lincoln's Inn. He may be late.'

'No one knows I'm sure,' Mrs Toms said as she turned to leave the room, 'what my poor feet do suffer.'

I felt a brute.

'Look, Mrs Toms. Perhaps I could get away early from the office, and pick up the ice on my way back.'

'No. I'll go round to Mr Barrett.' She was now in her role of a patient martyr.

'I'll go in a taxi on my way back from the office. Don't you bother,' I said.

'I do bother. I can't help bothering. I'm that sort. When I was a girl, mother always used to say to me, mother did, "Elsie, you'll die of worrying, you will!" And mother knew, you see.'

I looked furtively at my watch, I was already late for an appointment.

'I'll collect it on my way back.'

'I haven't seen Mr Barrett for ever so long. It's not often I get the chance of going out. Work, work, work. All day long. Not much better when I get home neither, with Mr Toms and his weak stummick.'

I felt I was losing grip of the conversation.

'What is it you'd like to do, Mrs Toms?'

'Maizie needs a bit of a walk now and then, poor dumb creature. I know I don't have no right to go out just when I want to. I'm only a servant. I know that. I know my place if I know nothing else. You must give me that, Mr Richard. Whatever else I may not know. I do know my place. Now don't I?'

'Yes, Mrs Toms. But . . .'

'It isn't as if I didn't look after you carefully, now is it?'

'No, Mrs Toms.'

'I do everything I can for you.'

'I know you do, Mrs Toms.'

'It isn't a big thing I'm asking, I'm sure.'

Tears were imminent. I took a deep breath.

'What is it, Mrs Toms?'

'It would give Maizie a walk and save you the taxi and give me a change just for once, if I could go round and fetch the ice from Mr Barrett.'

'Of course you can. I thought you didn't want to go.'

'Me not want to go? Whatever put that idea into your head?'

The ice appeared, and it was a pleasant party. I wished Tony had come. However, the next morning when she brought up breakfast Mrs Toms was bursting with information.

'Did Mr Tony turn up last night?' she demanded in her parade-ground voice.

'I'm afraid not.'

'Ah! That's because of those terrible exams he's working for.'

'Did you see him?'

'Not exactly. But I heard about him from Mr Barrett. Ever so nice, Mr Barrett is. He doesn't say much about it, but he's what I call reely a religious man. Ought to have been a parson, I told him yesterday. And he's that strong too. I saw him take a nut and crush it between the fingers of one hand. I saw it with my very own eyes. And that niece of his what's staying there till she can find a position, why she's such a sweet, shy little thing, Vera is. It made me cry just to look at her.'

'How old is she?'

'Only a girl, you know, but ever so well brought up. Sixteen I should say. Mr Barrett says that though she isn't getting paid while she's there, she helps him ever so about the house. Keeping a house clean isn't as easy as it looks, Mr Richard. I don't wonder Mr Barrett is glad of someone to help him. I don't like to complain, Mr Richard. And I'm not the complaining sort. Now am I, Mr Richard?'

'No, Mrs Toms.'

'Mother always used to say to me, mother did, "Now Elsie, complaining won't get you far any-where!" And mother was right, you see. Mother was a wonderful woman and I'm doing all I can to be like her. I never complain. But truth is truth all the world over. And it's no good not telling the truth. Now is it, Mr Richard?'

'No, Mrs Toms.'

'And it's only fair to you, Mr Richard, and to me, to tell you that keeping this house clean is more than one pair of hands can do properly.'

'But we've only got four rooms.'

'It isn't the rooms, Mr Richard. It's the dust. It's terrible. You sweep over a room. And the next instant, there it is full of dust again. Sweep, sweep, sweep. Work, work, work. There's no end to it. And no one knows, I'm sure, how my poor feet do suffer.'

'You must take things easy, Mrs Toms.'

'I daresay I should. Perhaps I'll lie down for a bit after lunch and try and rest myself? You won't mind, will you, Mr Richard, if I try and rest myself?'

'Of course not, Mrs Toms.'

'Good morning, Mr Richard.'

'Good morning, Mrs Toms.'

That afternoon Tony telephoned to ask me to go round for a drink after supper. Barrett's niece opened the door. I got a glimpse of a pale face and large brown eyes. As I walked upstairs I tried to interpret the expression I had seen flash across her face as she watched me. It was either frightened or furtive.

Tony was in high spirits.

'Barrett's mulled some claret. It's delicious. You must help me finish these cheese-cakes. Barrett made them. And he'll be offended if we don't finish them.'

'How is Sally?'

'My dear man, you have a fatal instinct of asking precisely the question one doesn't want asked. Well, if you want to know, I haven't seen her since we last met. She's taken up a ridiculous attitude to Barrett. And I really don't see why she should interfere with my domestic arrangements.'

'Domestic arrangements? Really, Tony,' I said laughing. 'You sound like a dowager.'

'I'm not perfect, I know. But at least I'm not smug.' His voice trembled with bitterness. I was astonished. I stared at him. Then our eyes met, and we both managed to laugh. But during the rest of the evening I think we were both self-conscious, and conversation was awkward.

CHAPTER FIVE

I did not see Tony for a month. I knew we would meet at the annual reunion dinner for the officers of our Regiment. I like Regimental reunions. But I think in Yeomanry Regiments, where the division between officers and men is transitory, it is a mistake to prolong the difference into civilian life.

'After all,' I said to Tony as we sat next to each other drinking down whatever was poured into our glasses by the waiter. 'After all,' I repeated rather drunkenly, 'take the chaps who were commissioned from our ranks to become officers in another Regiment. Why shouldn't they be here tonight?'

We stood up to drink a toast. When we sat down Tony said, 'You're getting rather opinionated in your old age, aren't you?'

'Rot.' I took a swig of brandy. 'If you want to know,' I said confidentially, 'I've always been fonder of the men. Some of my fellow-officers bore me stiff.'

'Stop being so bloody democratic. You know it's bogus.'

'Let's talk about something else. How's the law?'

'It's a bloody grind. I've passed the preliminary exams, now I've got the Final. My dear man, you've no idea what a grind I find it. In fact if it wasn't for Barrett I think I'd give up and buy a farm or something. Why don't you like him?'

'I just don't. I think he's undermining you.'

We stood up for another toast.

'I could get rid of him tomorrow if I wanted to. But I don't. He insulates me from a cold, drab world.'

'Perhaps it isn't a good thing to be insulated.'

'He provides comfort and warmth and food.'

'There's more to life than that.'

'Such as?'

I was going to say, 'things of the spirit', but I changed my mind.

'Sex.'

Tony laughed. 'No, he doesn't provide that. Though I daresay he would if I gave him half a chance. But I don't need sex all that much. I'd far rather have a good meal and go to bed early.'

'Things of the mind, then.'

'Barrett's not a fool, you know. He's quite interesting when you get to know him.'

I chuckled. 'I suppose you have long discussions on Proust.'

'I bet you he could do *The Times* crossword puzzle quicker than you could.'

'You don't mean to say you do crosswords together?'

'Why not?'

I could see that Tony was furious with me for laughing at him, but I was too drunk to care.

'Do you mean that you and Barrett solemnly sit together in the basement doing crossword puzzles?'

'Yes.'

'What about that little girl that opened the door for me? Is she still there?'

'Yes.'

'I thought she was going to get a job.'

'Her health isn't all that good. And I don't mind paying for her food, provided she helps Barrett around the house.'

'Does she like crosswords too?'

'Yes.' Tony had turned very pale. I should have stopped laughing.

'What a party!' I said.

I could see how much my laughter hurt him, and I was glad.

'Crosswords in the servants' hall!' I jeered.

Tony got up. 'My dear man, I can just put up with cracking snobs,' he said, 'but I'm not awfully keen on bloody hypocrites. You always pretend you're so wonderfully democratic. Let's mix the officers and men, and all that rot. But at heart you are the greatest snob I know. And quite honestly you make me sick.'

Against the black of his dinner jacket his face looked white and bloated. The curly fair hair which tumbled about his head seemed to have no connection with the mask it encircled, so that it looked like a golden wig stuck on the pate of an old actor. With a slow, pompous gesture he adjusted his tie. His hands were trembling. Then he turned away.

At one end of the hall, a group of young officers had started to sing. I joined them.

In Mobile: in Mobile.
Oh the eagles they fly high in Mobile.
Oh the eagles they fly high,
And they drop right in your eye—
Aren't you glad that you and I aren't in Mobile?
In Mobile: in Mobile
There's a one-eyed whore called Dinah in Mobile
There's a one-eyed whore called Dinah . . .

The idiotic song evoked a whole series of memories of army life; route marches in England, the words shouted joyously into the crisp air of a winter morning; concerts on board the troop ship, and later a walk round deck on a hot starry night; troop parties in the desert, an oil lamp glowing in the corner of the bivouac; our leave train to Alexandria, the words shouted defiantly, as if the volume of noise could help one to forget those who were no longer there. And in all those memories it was Tony who was by my side. He strode along the road in the pale sunshine; he watched the moon glittering in the water; he crawled under the tarpaulin into the smoky bivouac; he danced ludicrously in Alexandria. My eyes filled with tipsy tears. I looked round the hall for him. I found him standing by himself, pretending to examine a picture. I walked up to him. 'I'm a cracking snob,' I said, 'and you are a comfort-loving bastard, and now let's go and have a drink.'

'My dear man,' he said seizing my hand, 'my dear man.'

Then he looked down so that I should not see how moved he was. I wonder who began the gag that the English are unemotional?

We took a taxi round to his club, and my memory is blurred about the rest of our conversation. But I can remember walking home with Tony arm in arm, humming German carols. When we got outside his house in Benson Street, he flung out his arms dramatically.

'I have an important announcement to make which will give you the greatest of pleasure. The Barretts of Benson Street, uncle and niece, niece and uncle, are away.'

'Where have they gone to?'

'They wanted to visit their relatives in Manchester. So I gave them the week-end off. Do come in for a drink? I don't feel a bit sleepy, do you?'

'If I have one more drink I'd fall flat on my face.'

'I can put you up for the night. Do come in.'

'No, thanks awfully, Tony,' I said after a pause. 'I think I'd better go home.'

'Not one lil drink?'

'Not one.'

'Well, my dear man, God bless you.'

'God bless Tony.'

'Cheerio, old cock!' he called after me.

Six months later Tony told me what happened that night. I give his account here in order to preserve the sequence of events.

Tony decided to have a whisky and soda before going to bed. He took a bottle of whisky out of the drink cupboard. But he could not find the siphon. Still clutching the bottle he walked downstairs to the basement. He had forgotten to turn on the stair light, and for a while he fumbled for the switch. At last he found it and flicked on the light. At the opposite end of the kitchen, the door leading to the room occupied by Barrett's niece was open, and she was standing in the doorway, shivering in her nightdress.

'Oh, Mr Tony! What a fright you did give me! I thought it was a burglar.'

Tony laughed. 'Jolly brave of you to come in, Vera! More than I'd have done. Have a drink?'

'Oh, no thank you, sir.'

'Do stop looking so frightened. Come on. Let me give you a drink. It won't hurt you.'

'Well, perhaps just a drop.'

He found the siphon and poured out two whiskies. He was feeling warm and contented.

'Cheers.'

'And yours, sir,' she whispered.

He thought she looked quite sweet as she took nervous little sips at her drink.

'I thought you and Barrett had gone to Manchester?'

He could see the firm shape of her breasts through the thin material of her wrap.

'I didn't feel that good,' she whispered. 'So Mr Barrett's gone off by himself.'

'He left you by yourself?'

'Yes.'

A weight of emotion pressed down on him so that he could hardly breathe.

'We're alone here, I mean,' he said thickly.

'Yes.'

He felt he had lost control of reality. The plates on the dresser and the two cups on the sideboard seemed part of another world. A tap was dripping into the sink. Each drop fell at regular intervals like the beat of a metronome. He was breathing heavily. It worried him that his breath did not keep time with the drips. He could hear the two sounds cutting across the stillness of the room. She must have noticed his emotion when she raised her eyes to his. At that moment a tide of passion swept over him, and the room turned black before his eyes. It was as if he had given his sight to increase his sense of touch, for he felt intensely aware in all his limbs. He felt his arms encircle her waist and crush her body to him. He felt his lips on her skin searching for the moist softness of her mouth. Then with a spasm of joy he felt her tongue sliding through his lips and her hands stroking his hair. They stumbled through the door to her little room. He remembered nothing more until he awoke feeling sick.

He was in a strange bedroom. Then with a shudder of remorse he recognised it. She was still with him. He began to get out of the bed cautiously in order to avoid waking her. But she was awake already. She was lying on her back staring at him with large brown eyes. She had thrown back the coverlet, and he could see her slender body and her small uptilted breasts. Her nipples were crimson and erect. She smiled up at him. She took his hand and drew it to her body.

'Once more,' she said.

CHAPTER SIX

I have tried to piece the scene together from the halting phrases which Tony used when he told me about it six months later.

'At first,' he said, 'I was haunted by the idea of Barrett finding out.'

'Did you tell her that?'

'Oh yes, I told her everything. You see by then I was mad about her.'

'What did she say?'

Apparently she reassured him.

'If you don't tell him,' she used to say, 'you can bet your life that I won't. He'd never get over it.'

He was wildly in love with her. It was as if passion had been an animal asleep yet growing in his body. Vera had awoken the animal which now gnawed at his heart. It controlled him utterly, and it was insatiable. No sooner was his passion slaked than it was aroused again with increased appetite.

She told him it was dangerous for her to come up to his room until Barrett, whose room lay the other side of the basement, had gone to bed.

'I can't come every night, dear. It wouldn't be safe.'

At night he would lie in bed staring up at the ceiling, tortured by desire for her lean body. There was always the chance that she would come. He could think of nothing else. Gradually his habits changed. He used to lunch near the lecture rooms. But now he would dash back for a quick meal so as to get a glimpse of her. After lunch one day, he was about to leave the house in time for the afternoon lectures when he saw Barrett walking out of the house with a suit under his arm. He remembered he had told him to get it cleaned and pressed. For a moment he stared after him. Then he stepped slowly down the stairs to the basement. His mouth was dry, and he could feel his heart thudding. There was no one in the kitchen. He knocked softly on Vera's door and opened it. She was lying on her bed resting. She started violently as he came in.

'He's gone out, Vera. We're alone, my darling. We're alone, my darling. We're all alone. Oh Vera! I love you so much.'

She did not answer. But she began trembling. Her whole body shook as if with a fever. He sat down on the bed beside her.

'What is it, my darling?'

'Quick,' she said, 'quick.'

For the first time he knew the ecstasies of passion fully requited. All day long he could think of nothing but Vera. He gave up going to lectures because he could not concentrate. He took law books home from the library; but he did not read them. He waited in an agony of impatience for Barrett to leave the house. Sometimes Vera would go out with him, and the anguish would be prolonged. It seemed to him that she was going out with Barrett more often than before.

'I never get you alone in the afternoons now. Why don't you stay in?'

'I think he's beginning to get suspicious.' Fear clouded his heart.

'You swear that whatever happens you'll never tell him.'

'Of course I won't, silly.'

'God how I love you!'

'Come on, silly.'

He never paused to analyse why he was afraid of discovery by Barrett. I think it was probably because part of Tony disapproved. I daresay he suspected that his infatuation was rank lust. Tony was shocked, and therefore he supposed that Barrett would also be shocked.

Sometimes, after she had left him, he would vow that he would never lose control again. But then the image of her smooth, slender body and firm breasts would shine before his eyes, and his desire would rush back and overwhelm his will.

Meanwhile he forced himself to lead his usual gregarious life, partly because any change in routine might make Barrett suspicious, partly because in company he sometimes found relief from his torment. The excellent dinner parties for five or six continued as before. I went to one of them, and I must confess I noticed nothing unusual about Tony except that he was drinking more heavily than usual. I had a faint hope that I would see Sally. But I learnt later that she still refused to come to his house while Barrett was there. The parties became increasingly popular. Barrett was a perfect cook. He now appeared in a well-cut white coat for cocktail parties and an exquisite suit to serve the dinner he had so carefully cooked. His long, bony fingers gave deft twists to napkins and fashioned pastries into curious shapes. He was like a snake as he wound his way carefully across the crowded little room. I was always aware of his presence, and his tall sinuous body, his slimy face and his prim rosebud lips began to haunt my dreams.

Tony's attitude to him at this period was confused. He was proud of Barrett's skill and grateful to him for making his life comfortable. He needed Barrett's services more than ever. Yet he fiercely resented the need for his presence in the house. Barrett's prudish form, he felt, stood between him and his desire. Every day Barrett frustrated him. But above all, Tony felt guilty. Barrett slaved and scraped for him, and he was deceiving his loyal servant. Thus Tony would snap at him in the afternoon and apologise humbly when Barrett had returned from his walk.

Reading through the pages I have written, I realize that my description of Barrett is so inadequate that it hovers perilously close to being ludicrous. My only excuse is that there *was* something comic about Barrett. It was like looking at a fantastically shaped log and knowing that its other side was swarming with lice. His appearance was absurd, and I sometimes wanted to laugh at his voice. But my giggle ended with a shudder.

As the weeks passed by, the quality of Tony's passion changed. Periods of satisfied indifference when he felt calm and contented replaced the previous moments of remorse. The animal was dozing. Tony was left in peace. He could think of Vera with quiet, painless affection. Then, one afternoon, or perhaps as he lay in bed at night, the animal would turn over uneasily. His heart would begin to beat faster as the creature stirred into consciousness. Until, fully awakened, desire stroked his guts and clawed at his heart and his head and throat and took control over him so that his whole being was aflame with passion and he could scarcely stop himself clambering down the stairs and bursting into the room where lay the only object in the world into which he could plunge his pain and pour out its fierceness.

As the periods of indifference grew longer so did Tony's affection for Vera increase. He was grateful to her for sharing his passion, and sometimes he felt guilty for the eagerness of her response. He was devoted to her, and the fact that she was the niece of his servant added a poignancy to his devotion as the days passed by and the green buds pushed out to the watery sun and burgeoned into flower.

The crash came during the summer holidays.

Tony had realised that Vera must go with Barrett to Manchester to spend the holidays with their family. Without her Benson Street would be unbearable, so he decided to stay with his aunt in Cornwall. This meant that Benson Street would be empty for two weeks. He called on me the evening before the house was to be shut up and gave me a spare latchkey to the front door.

'You might keep an eye on it, will you? There's a good man. I don't like the idea of it being absolutely empty with all these robberies, but it can't be helped. I'll phone you as soon as I get back.'

A week later I happened to be passing along Benson Street after a party which had lasted until midnight. I looked up at Tony's house and thought I saw a light burning behind the curtain of his bedroom window, which was on the top floor. I decided that Tony must have returned from Cornwall sooner than he had expected. I walked on. Then I stopped. If so, why hadn't he telephoned me? Perhaps he had returned that evening and found me out. I stopped. Then I walked back to his house and opened the front door with my latchkey. The moonlight streamed into the narrow hall. There was no luggage or clothes to suggest that Tony had returned. I shut the door quietly, and crept up the stairs. None of the curtains had been drawn. Moonlight poured through the long windows. On the half-landing below Tony's room I paused. I could see a light under his door. I listened. I could hear nothing except the sound of my breath. Then I heard the bed creak, and a voice said, 'Hand us another cigarette.'

It was Barrett's voice.

'You've only just had one,' a girl's voice replied.

'Well, I want another,' Barrett said.

There was a pause. The bed creaked again.

'You don't want to smoke,' the girl said. 'You don't want to smoke, do you? Come on. Once more.'

'I'm tired out I tell you.'

'Come on. Once more.'

I began to creep away. A stairboard snapped. I stood still. My heart was thumping.

'There's someone there,' he said.

'Course there isn't.'

'You locked up didn't you?'

'Course I did.'

'You bolted the front door?'

'I didn't bolt it actually.'

'You bleeding little idiot.'

The door was flung open, and Barrett peered

out of the brightly lit room. He stepped quietly on to the landing. His long, thin body was green and horrible in the moonlight. Then he saw me. Neither of us spoke. Into the stillness the voice from the bedroom came like a blasphemy shrieked in chapel.

'There's no one there. I told you there wasn't. Come on back or you'll catch your death of cold. Come on, Hugo. If you come back now you can . . .'

The hot words tumbled about my ears as I ran down the stairs and rushed out of the house.

CHAPTER SEVEN

I dreaded having to tell Tony. But my main feeling, I confess, was satisfaction that at last Barrett's influence was broken. Tony telephoned me as soon as he got back. I asked him to come round to my house.

'If it's about Barrett, do you mind coming here?' he said. 'Because it's only fair on him to hear what you've got to say.'

'All right, I'll come right away.'

Tony opened the door to me. We sat down in the living room.

'Now let's hear what he's done.'

I told him what had happened. He turned very white. When I told him that Vera was in the room, he gave a long indrawn sigh of misery. For a while he was motionless. Then he strode to the bell pull and plunged it down violently. I could hear the bell echoing down in the basement. He was silent. I could think of nothing to say. Barrett appeared. He was perfectly calm.

'You rang, sahr?'

'Mr Merton says you were in my room with Vera.'

'That is so, sahr. May I see you alone for a few moments?'

'Would you like me to go, Tony?' I asked.

'No, please stay.'

I could see Tony struggling to control himself.

'You realise you have committed a criminal offence?'

'I fail to see why, sahr.'

'Because she's your niece, you dirty swine.'

Barrett winced. Then he said in his soft, oily voice, 'I'm afraid I lied to you, sahr. Vera is not my niece.'

'The police can find out about that.'

'You can ring up the police if you like. But I think you will find I am not the one who has committed any offence. You see my fiancée is only just sixteen.'

'You're mad. It's not true.'

Barrett's eyes glittered. He strolled to the door.

'Vera,' he called out, 'will you come in, dear, a minute.'

In silence we could hear her walking up the stairs. I was annoyed how calm she looked as she walked in.

'Now, Vera,' Barrett said, 'owing to Mr Tony's attitude I'm afraid I must ask you to tell them our little secret. Come on now. Don't be shy. Tell them.'

'Hugo and I are going to be married,' she whispered.

'It's not true, Vera,' Tony blurted out. 'For God's sake say it's not true.'

'Of course it's true. You never wanted to marry me, did you? You can't always have everything just as you like, you know. Come on Hugo,' she said looking spitefully at me. 'I don't like being stared at.'

In silence they left the room. Then Tony began to cry, with long racking sobs. It was later that evening when he had moved into my house that he told me the story which I have already set down.

CHAPTER EIGHT

Mrs Toms was delighted that Tony was staying at Oakley Street. 'Oh he's ever so poorly,' she kept on saying. 'Now what he needs is a proper long rest. I do wonder at that nice Mr Barrett leaving him, I reely do.'

We had decided to tell our friends that Barrett had given notice to take a better job. The warm protective feeling I had about Tony found expression during those first few weeks. He had let his house furnished, and I was delighted that he was staying with me. Mrs Toms and I tried to make him as comfortable as we could. But Tony found it hard to rest. His nerves were still strained from the war, and he was drinking too much. He procured the whisky he drank from his own wine merchant so I had no obvious reason to complain, even if I had so ventured, for he was touchy to criticism. I decided to leave him alone until he was stronger. One evening he came back from Lincoln's Inn looking exhausted. The crisp, golden hair fell about the face of a corpse. He went straight to the sideboard and poured himself out a tumblerful of whisky. Then he turned round to find me watching him.

'For Christ's sake don't look so smug.'

'You can drink yourself sick for all I care.'

'Oh, I am sorry, my dear man,' he said later, 'I'm a cracking bore these days. I don't know what's wrong with me.'

I was not going to let him escape as easily as that.

'There are two main things wrong with you,' I said. 'Drink and self-indulgence.'

'Oh to hell with you and your bloody moralising! It's enough to drive one to drink.'

However, gradually Tony got better. A faint colour touched his white cheeks. His eyes lost their look of haggard anxiety. I decided to make the first move in my campaign. I struck at breakfast.

'By the way, Sally Grant is coming in for a drink this evening,' I said casually.

'I think I shall be out,' he said. 'Give her my love.'

However, he appeared in the living room at six, and I noticed he had changed his clothes. Sally was looking lovelier than ever. I was grateful to her for playing her part so well. She appeared gay and feckless. She did not mention Barrett. I, for my part, made some extremely strong cocktails and kept up my end of our inane chatter, and I absent-mindedly got rather drunk. At last Tony reacted as I had hoped.

'Where are you dining, Sally?'

'At home with the family.'

'Can't you ring up and say you are dining with us?'

'Oh yes, please, do, Sally,' I said.

'I'd love to,' she said.

Half an hour later I saw them out. The operation was working to schedule. Even my headache, I think, was quite convincing. At about midnight I heard Tony come in.

I lunched with Sally secretly the next day.

'Well?'

'It's no use. No use at all.'

'He was drunk.'

'Oh, it wasn't that. It's hard to explain. But somehow I felt when I was talking to him that he wasn't really there. It was just a body that was opposite me. The mind had gone. I felt I was talking to an empty hulk. Oh, Richard, what has happened to him?'

'What did you talk about?'

'Friends, parties, theatres. Anything except what really mattered.'

'Did he say anything about Barrett?'

'Nothing, except when we were driving home in the taxi he mumbled something about habit.'

'Can you remember his words?'

'Something about wanting things one more time. You want one more drink, and one more night to live. You always want things once more. Richard, why did Barrett leave?'

'To get a better job.'

'Where?'

'In Manchester.'

'You're not a good liar, Richard. Besides I saw him creeping along Sloane Street a few days ago.'

'Perhaps he was on holiday.'

'All right. Lie if you must.'

The next evening Tony left the house at seven. I did not ask where he was going. At two in the morning I was awakened by someone knocking at the front door.

It was Tony, white and swaying.

'Awfully sorry,' he muttered. 'I seem to have lost my key.'

There were smears of lipstick about his cheeks, and he reeked of cheap scent. He was very drunk. I helped him upstairs.

'I'm unclean,' he kept muttering.

The next morning he left to stay with his aunt.

'I must get away from London,' he said. 'It'll be clean in the country.'

CHAPTER NINE

I was delighted with the improvement in Tony's health when he returned from the country two months later. I was especially relieved to see him fit and steady because my firm was sending me to the United States, probably for a year. I lunched with Sally. She was radiant with happiness.

'I know why the country did him so much good,' she said.

'You see, Barrett never went with him to the country, so there was nothing in Cornwall to remind him of the odious creature.'

The weeks before I left passed pleasantly. Tony had begun to work for his Bar Final. He seldom stayed out late. He and Sally would dine early in Chelsea. He would see her home and then join me for a night-cap. When I sailed I reckoned I might soon get a cable to say they were engaged. Tony had moved back to his house, taking Mrs Toms to look after him until my return. I had let Oakley Street furnished. I learned the next part of the story from letters I received while in the States. The first was from Mrs Toms:

'Just a line to say that all is O.K. here except

the geyser is wrong and poor Maizie is in trouble. The fishmonger called with a bill, the impudence of it, and Maizie went for him, brave little dog. She did not bite him real bad but he carried on something terrible. I told him it was only just a little blood that is all. But he said as he would tell the Police and have my Maizie put away the poor dumb creature what never harmed anyone in all her life. Except him of course. Mother always said that little men make the most trouble, and mother was always right.

I was ever so upset. I told Mr Tony. He is a real gentleman. He's gone round to the fishmonger and everything is settled. It is a pleasure to work for Mr Tony. Nothing is too good for him.

The weather is damp and my poor feet are something terrible. Hoping you are having a nice time.

Yours truly,
Mrs Toms.'

A letter from Sally later mentioned this incident . . .

'. . . Tony is fine. Mrs Toms dotes on him all the more after l'affaire du Fishmonger. Tony had quite a business settling it. But finally he and the fishmonger became the greatest buddies. And the fishmonger insisted on taking Tony out to a favourite pub of his for a drink. And guess who Tony ran into in the pub. Barrett! Who apparently told him some fantastic story which Tony has swallowed completely the poor dope . . .'

Then I heard from Tony:

'. . . The other night I was at the pub when I spotted Barrett. I pretended not to see him. But he came up to me. I think he was a little bit tight. I wasn't too sober. He kept saying how sorry he was he had "deceived me" and "played me false" and would I please listen to his explanation. He was absurdly melodramatic. People in the pub were beginning to turn round and stare at us. I was afraid that at any moment he was going to kneel down and weep. He was madly keen I should hear his story. So I just had to listen.

It appears he was crazy about Vera before he came to work for me. And he thought she was keen about him. They were saving up money to get married. But her father ill-treated her, and he wanted to get her away from home. He couldn't bear to think of her suffering. It seems her father was rather a brute. At any rate Barrett had to pay him quite a bit to consent. She was only fifteen, so he couldn't marry her. But he'd got to find a home for her. That was why he lied to me and told me she was his niece.

He knew nothing about my affair with Vera until that last morning. But he said that now he knows her better he's not a bit surprised. He's found out that she's a complete nymphomaniac. Anything in trousers will do. He told me that you'd heard something of her style the night you broke in on them. She's run off with a bookie, taking some of Barrett's money with her.

At any rate that's his story. And I must say it sounds as if I'd done him wrong, rather than vice versa. Poor Barrett! He looked so prim and pale! He's looking after an old lady in Lowndes Square. She rings the bell all day long, and he is quite miserable. Do you know of anyone who wants a really first-class manservant? For two pins I'd take him back myself . . .'

I replied by postcard:

'Dear Tony,

Yesterday I jumped off the top of the Waldorf Astoria and landed safely on the sidewalk. The day before that I rode on a dromedary from New York to San Francisco in seven hours; I'd have done it in six hours but I had to stop to change a shoe. This morning I was elected President of the United States. I reckon you will believe all this, because if you believe Barrett's story you'll believe anything. Love,

Richard.'

I did not hear from Tony again for a month.

'. . . I know you are going to mind this no end. But I can't help it. Mrs Toms was beginning to get on my nerves. She never will stop talking, bless her. And though I know you don't care, you must admit she can't cook. Besides the chance of getting Barrett back was too good to miss. So I've given her a month's pay and she leaves at the end of this week. She's perfectly happy. She'll find temporary work until you come back, which I hope will be soon, you wretched man!

I'm not going to try and explain about B. except to promise you that you're wrong. I had a long talk with him a week ago. I'm sure he was telling the truth. I feel I've done him a great injustice.

Sally, I'm afraid, is being maddening about it. But I'm tired of having other people run my life. I only hope she'll come to see my point of view. I can't tell you how much I look forward to B's return and being able to lead a civilised existence again. Incidentally he tells me that Vera has married her bookie so that's one complication out of the way.'

I wrote him a violent letter but I knew it was hopeless.

Two months later I heard from Sally.

'. . . This is just to say good-bye. Hamish Campbell has asked me to marry him. We're leaving for his farm in Rhodesia. I've told him pretty well everything, and he understands. Richard, please don't think too harshly of me. It wouldn't have been any good. Richard, please send me your good wishes. They would mean so much to me. . . .'

What could I do but wish her all the luck in the world?

CHAPTER TEN

I fear that the weakness of this story is that I am unable to explain the reason for the increase in Barrett's influence during the year I was away. He stood for ease and comfort in Tony's mind. But it must have been more than that. The only explanation I can offer is tenuous. I think that the picture of Tony becoming a slave to his comfort is incomplete. For what is comfort? The effortless satisfaction of one's needs, easy fulfilment. But there are needs beyond food, warmth and amusement. Tony was lonely. The screen of convention which stood between him and Barrett had been shattered. There was now an easy understanding. The barriers were down. They had been after the same girl. They were no longer master and servant. Both were still bachelors. Both were lonely. And thus Barrett gradually became the dragoman who could be trusted to bring Tony safely whatever he needed.

Barrett was far too clever to state the position as baldly as I have done. I expect he took on his role of dragoman step by step, with sly little hints and furtive allusions, until he finally established his position as the agent who satisfied Tony's needs. He became comfort incarnate.

My explanation may be wrong, but it certainly tallies with what I discovered when I returned to England a year later. I returned in December.

As soon as I got home I telephoned Tony. There was no reply. I spent the next day with Mrs Toms tidying my house, which the tenants had left in a filthy state. There was still no reply from Tony's number. Mrs Toms was certain he was in London, so after tea I decided to walk round. It was a bleak, rainy evening, and the narrow roads glittered in the lamplight. A taxi was slithering slowly along Benson Street like a solitary ship in a canal. There was a light in the basement of number 7. I rang the front-door bell. Presently I heard the sound of the bolts being drawn back, and Barrett opened the door. He was wearing a tightly fitting blue suit and a bright green tie which made him look like an undertaker out on a spree.

'Mr Tony is in the kitchen,' he said. 'Allow me to show you the way.'

Tony was sitting in a shabby armchair. I was dismayed by the change in him. He had grown fat, almost gross. There were puffy bags of flesh under his eyes, and his skin was rough and mottled. A book fell from his knees when he stood up to greet me. I saw the little black and white squares of a crossword puzzle on the cover.

'Hello, Richard, where have you sprung from?

We sit down here because it's warmer and so much more comfortable. What will you drink, my dear man? Whisky?'

I noticed a decanter and glasses on the dresser.

'Whisky, please.'

He poured out large dollops into glasses. His hands were trembling uncontrollably. He splashed in some soda clumsily.

'Look out or you'll waste it,' Barrett said.

'There's more where it comes from,' Tony said with a nervous laugh. 'Cheers.'

'Cheers.'

A silence fell. I could think of nothing to say. My loathing of Barrett almost suffocated me.

'Did you have a good time in the States?'

I turned my back on Barrett. My account of New York sounded inane. Once more there was silence which was broken by Barrett.

'I wonder if we can interest Mr Merton in our pastime,' he said with a snigger. 'Do crossword puzzles interest you, Mr Merton?'

'They bore me stiff.'

'They are our favourite occupation,' Tony said quickly.

I stood up to go.

'Can you dine with me tonight, Tony?'

I felt Barrett was looking at him.

'I'm afraid I can't.'

'Tomorrow then.'

'That's no good either.'

'What about Thursday?'

'May I give you a ring and let you know?'

'Will you see me out?' I wanted to see him alone.

'I'm afraid Tony's had a bad chill,' Barrett said. He was openly hostile now. 'I can't possibly allow him out into the cold.'

'Will you see me out, Tony?'

'Excuse me, won't you, my dear man? But I've not been well.'

'I'm asking you to see me out, Tony.'

I could hardly bear to look at the pain of his defeat.

'Sorry, Richard.' He looked pathetic as he stared up at Barrett.

'Good night, then.'

I ran quickly up the stairs and out of the house. As I marched along the gleaming pavements, I tried to think where I had seen that expression on his face before. The next morning I remembered. It was in an old photograph I'd come across once in his desk. Tony aged about ten was looking up at the worn face of a kindly woman.

'Who was that, Tony,' I asked.

'Oh, that was the favourite woman of my life. I think she was the only person who really loved me when I was a child. She would have given me anything in the world if she could.'

'But who was she?'

'My Nanny.'

CHAPTER ELEVEN

Tony did not telephone me, and there was no reply to his number. I wondered how I could get hold of him. On Friday night I stayed late at my club. I could not get a taxi, so I decided to walk to an Underground station. Few people were loitering in Piccadilly because it was bitterly cold. I was sorry for the prostitutes. I saw one of them accost a sailor. In his warm coat he could afford to loiter. But she was shivering. He looked at her face and then abruptly turned away. She glanced quickly about to see that no policeman was watching her and then walked hastily after him. She called out softly to him, but I could not hear what she was saying. He strode on without giving her a look. In her high-heeled shoes she could not keep up with him. She turned round wearily. Then she spotted me and sidled towards me. It was not until she was quite close that we recognised each other. It was Vera. The large brown eyes peered out of a garish, wizened face. She looked desperately ill.

'Mr Richard,' she said. 'It's Mr Richard.'

I had four pounds on me. I handed them to her. I could not bear to see her look so ill.

'Oh, I couldn't. Oh, Mr Richard, you always were kind. How is he? How is Tony?' She was shivering.

'He's all right.'

'Why doesn't he answer my letters? I know it isn't right to ask for money. But he was always generous.'

'I didn't know you'd written.'

'I didn't. Not at first.'

'Why doesn't your husband help you?'

'My husband?'

'I thought you were married?'

'Me? Never.'

'I thought you'd left Barrett to marry a bookmaker.'

'What a bloody lie,' she screamed out. 'So that's what he says, is it, the dirty swine.'

Passers-by were staring at us. I looked at my watch. Every bar would be shut.

'Where can we go to talk?'

'What about my place? It's only a room. But it's warm.'

'All right.'

She lived in a dingy street running off Shaftesbury Avenue. We climbed up a sour smelling staircase to a tiny little room on the fourth floor. The sheets on the double bed were filthy, and the grey blankets were thrown back in disorder. An empty gin bottle stood amongst the litter of makeup on the dressing-table. There was no other furniture except a kitchen chair, on which I sat. She put a shilling in the meter and lit the gas fire.

'I could make some tea if you'd like some. Sorry I've got nothing stronger to offer.'

'I'd like some tea.'

So we were drinking tea while she told me in disconnected scraps of events the outline of her seventeen years of life.

Her mother died when she was young, and her father, who was a clerk in a solicitor's office in Manchester, looked after her. He appears to have been a weak, nervous little man who was kind to her except when he got drunk or when he had to pay out money on her clothes. 'He was very mean,' Vera told me. She was the only child, so she found school exciting after the loneliness of her home, and she did well at work. It was after her fourteenth birthday that Barrett first came to the house.

'I didn't like him. Not one little bit. He used to look at me with those cold eyes of his as if he was trying to make up his mind about something.'

'How had he met your father?'

'I don't know. He was in service at the time. I know that. I never did find out what the two of them were up to. But all that year they were as thick as thieves. Hugo used to bring Dad little presents. Sometimes it would be cigars or a bottle of whisky. Sometimes it would be tickets for the theatre and we'd all three go together. When I was fifteen I was taken away from school. I can remember how I cried. But Dad said we were going to the seaside for a holiday with Mr Barrett.'

She put down her cup, and leaned back on her pillow. The fingers of her hands never stopped writhing together.

'Hugo told me later how much he paid Dad for me. He paid him thirty pounds. Apart from the presents, of course. But there wasn't to be any force about it, Dad said. Always a gent, Dad was. Oh, but Hugo was clever. He did it all so gradually. Except the last part. But by then he'd caught me, and anyway I was drunk.'

She raised herself on one elbow.

'I've known a few men since then,' she said. 'And I'll tell you he was the queerest. Of course I didn't know any better then. You can get used to almost anything, I always say. If you really want to know I came to need it, see? I'd have done anything for him. It was he who put me up to Tony. The poor duck gave himself away every time he looked at me. "It suits my book," Hugo said. "He might send you away otherwise."'

'What happened after he was sacked?'

'He chucked me. That's what happened. He'd found another girl, see. He only likes them young.'

'You know you could go to the police.'

'You see what I am. Do you think they'd take my word against his? Besides I'm afraid. You don't know what he did to me when I came back for money.'

'Would you like to train for some job? I can give you a bit of money to get on with.'

'Oh, you're kind, Mr Richard. Really you are. I'd do anything for you. Anything. Do you know that? Anything.'

'What could you train for?'

But she was no longer listening. A change had come over her whole being. Her face was flushed, and her eyes, which seemed to have grown larger, were staring at me. She was breathing heavily.

'Anything I'd do. Anything for you. You're a man, aren't you? Don't be afraid. Come on, Richard.'

I got up.

'I'm afraid I must go.'

'Not yet. Stay a little while.' She was panting now.

'I must go.'

'Just a little while.'

All her body was trembling.

'Good night, Vera.'

'Stay. You must stay.'

She clutched my hand. 'Come on. Can't you see? Quickly. Quickly.'

I tore myself free, and opened the door.

'You bloody sod!' she shrieked at the top of her voice. 'Call yourself a man, do you? Call yourself a man?'

I could still hear her screaming as I left the house.

CHAPTER TWELVE

The next evening the fog was so thick that I had to grope my way to Benson Street. Fog filled my throat and nostrils and seeped through my clothes so that I could feel it like icy glue round my body. I remembered to go to the back door. Barrett answered the bell. For a moment I thought he was going to try to stop me coming in. I strode past him, and he followed me to the kitchen. Tony made no attempt to disguise his displeasure at seeing me.

'What do you want?' he demanded. He was slightly drunk.

I made myself as pleasant to Barrett as I could.

'I'm awfully sorry to butt in,' I said smiling at him. 'I thought I'd like to join the two of you for a little drink, if you could stand me one.'

Tony looked at his watch and then at Barrett.

'It's a pleasure I'm sure,' Barrett said with a smirk. 'But I hope you'll excuse us if we don't ask you to stay after seven. You see we're expecting visitors.'

'I only dropped in for a few minutes.'

I made small talk while Tony poured out drinks.

Then I said casually, 'By the way, what news of Vera?'

'Still abroad with her bookie, I suppose,' Tony said.

'Have you had any news of her, Barrett?'

'I had a postcard a few weeks ago. From Nice it was. Do you remember my telling you, Tony? She's there with a man.'

My chance had come. I stood up.

'Vera has been a prostitute in London for the last nine months,' I said slowly. 'I saw her last night. Tony, please let me see you alone. Please.'

Tony stared at me with bloodshot eyes. I could hear the kitchen clock ticking. He turned to Barrett.

'Why did you lie to me?'

'I wanted to spare your feelings.'

'Let me see you alone, Tony.'

'She's told him a pack of lies,' Barrett cut in quickly, 'and if he believes her, the more fool him.'

'You're a liar. And you know it,' I said. There was a pause.

'I'm sure I'm not going to stay here to be insulted,' Barrett said suddenly in a high-pitched querulous voice and stalked out of the room.

Then I repeated every word of Vera's story. Tony listened in silence.

'Don't you see that in each case he destroys his victims from within? He helps them destroy themselves by serving their particular weakness. In Vera's case it was lust. In her father's case it was avarice. In your case it began by being plain love of comfort. I don't think it's much more than that even now, is it? Is it, Tony?'

His eyes were haggard as he stared at me.

'It's more than that now,' he said. 'You know it is.'

In the stillness we both heard the key turn in the lock of the back door. Someone was coming in. The door opened, and a young girl pranced into the kitchen. Her face was inexpertly rouged, and her waist and emaciated hands were tiny. She looked like a child dressed up in her mother's clothes.

'Good evening all,' she said. Then she noticed me. 'Oh, we've got company, I see. Won't you introduce me?'

Tony turned round. 'Now perhaps you understand,' he said. He gulped down his drink and poured himself another.

'Aren't you going to introduce me, Tony?' she asked.

I shook her hand. 'My name's Richard Merton,' I said. 'Pleased to meet you.'

'The pleasure's mine, I'm sure.'

'Haven't you seen enough?' Tony asked. 'Can't you see it's hopeless?'

'What's up with you?' the girl asked. 'You asked me to come, didn't you?'

At that moment Barrett walked in.

'Hallo there,' she said. 'I was beginning to think I'd come the wrong evening.'

'You'll be coming to a different place next time,' Barrett said pettishly. 'I'm not going to stay here to be insulted.'

'Who's insulted you, duckie?' she asked taking off her coat.

She was wearing a thin blouse which showed the shape of her young breasts.

'Put on your coat. We're not staying here.'

'Who said not? You want me to stay, Tony, don't you?'

She took his hand and began caressing it. Then she drew it to her breast.

'It's for him to choose,' Barrett said. 'Either his friend goes or we go.'

Tony stared miserably at the worn carpet. He was silent.

'It's all right, Tony,' I said, 'I'll go. God bless you. Good night.'

I left the room at once so they should not see my misery. I walked heavily down the short passage to the back door. I felt so exhausted that every movement was an effort. My hands trembled as I groped for the latch. Suddenly the kitchen door swung open, and Tony walked out. He stood absolutely still staring at me.

'I couldn't bear to see you go like that,' he said at length.

'That's all right,' I managed to say.

Suddenly I felt his arm round my shoulder. Then he withdrew it again, as if he had done something wrong.

'Oh, Richard,' he said brokenly. 'Oh, my dear Richard. Don't leave me. I'm unclean. I know I am. But don't leave me.'

'Come with me then.'

He was silent. There was no sound from the kitchen. They were obviously listening.

'I'll do all I can to make you happy,' I said softly.

His bloodshot eyes were full of tears.

'Come with me.'

He stood swaying on his feet, staring at me.

Barrett's high-pitched voice broke the silence.

'We're waiting for you, Tony,' he called out. 'We're both waiting for you.'

There was a furtive giggle, then a little gasp, a whimper, then silence. Tony flushed. He began to tremble all over.

'Come with me,' I urged.

But he was no longer listening. He was breathing heavily, and his eyes were dilated. Then he broke away from me with a low cry and stumbled towards the kitchen door.

'I'm staying,' I heard him say in a thick voice. Then he turned round. For a moment our eyes met.

'Good-bye, Richard,' he said. 'Have a good time in prig's alley.'

'Good-bye, Tony.'

I opened the door and walked out into the cold darkness. The fog was so thick that sometimes I would get lost in stretches of deep blackness between the circles of light from the lamp-posts. I knew it would be a long journey before I reached home.